VOICES OF THE TROJAN WAR

KATE HOVEY

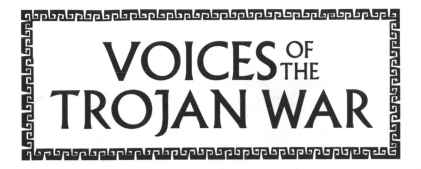

VOICES OF THE TROJAN WAR

with illustrations by
LEONID GORE

Margaret K. McElderry Books
New York London Toronto Sydney

The author wishes to thank Emma D. Dryden,
Elizabeth Harding, Peg Leavitt, Bobo Lee, Judith Pacht,
Candace Pearson, and Carol Tippit
for their guidance and support.

Margaret K. McElderry Books
An imprint of Simon & Schuster Children's Publishing Division
1230 Avenue of the Americas, New York, New York 10020
Text copyright © 2004 by Kate Hovey
Illustrations copyright © 2004 by Leonid Gore

Book design by Kristin Smith and Abelardo Martínez
The text for this book is set in Deepdene.
The illustrations for this book are rendered in acrylics on paper.
Manufactured in the United States of America
2 4 6 8 10 9 7 5 3 1
Library of Congress Cataloging-in-Publication Data
Hovey, Kate.
Voices of the Trojan War / Kate Hovey ; illustrated by Leonid Gore.—1st ed.
p. cm.
Summary: A collection of poems that give voice to the ancient Greeks and Trojans who
fought the Trojan War, a ten-year battle that ended when Greek warriors gained
entrance to the city in a large wooden horse.
ISBN 0-689-85768-3
1. Trojan War—Juvenile poetry. 2. Greece—History, Military—To 146 B.C.—
Juvenile poetry. 3. Troy (Extinct city)—Juvenile poetry. 4. Children's poetry, American.
[1. Trojan War—Poetry. 2. Greece—History, Military—To 146 B.C.—Poetry.
3. Troy (Extinct city)—Poetry. 4. American poetry.] I. Gore, Leonid, ill. II. Title.
PS3558.O8749V65 2004
811'.54—dc22
2003012606

FIRST
EDITION

For the Fallen

—K. H. and L. G.

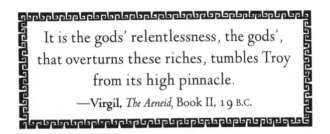

It is the gods' relentlessness, the gods',
that overturns these riches, tumbles Troy
from its high pinnacle.

—**Virgil**, *The Aeneid*, Book II, 19 B.C.

Invocation: Talking with the Muse

POET: Tell us, muse, of Troy's dark days;
                  of the House of Priam's fall;
            of Hector, the old king's bravest son,
                  killed at the Trojan wall.
            Sing of his daughter, the priestess Cassandra,
                  Apollo's tragic seer;
            sing of the fate she prophesied
                  that the Trojans refused to hear.

MUSE: *Stories told of gods and men*
            still echo in your ears,
            ancient voices drifting down
            vast corridors of years.

POET: Sing of their brother, the shepherd Paris;
            sing of the bride he stole—
            Helen, wife of the Spartan king—
                who yielded her heart and soul,

abandoning home and family,
    all for a handsome face.
Tell us, muse, of the Greek ships launched,
    avenging the king's disgrace.

MUSE: *Homer, Virgil, Aeschylus,*
              Ovid, Euripides—
              listen! No one living's heard
              voices as great as these.

POET: Sing of Achilles, the fiercest warrior
              to sail from the isles of Greece;
              of Ithaca's shrewd Odysseus,
              who fought, though he longed for peace.

MUSE: *Words repeated many times—*
              what is left to tell?
              Let the heroes speak themselves;
              ask the gods as well.

POET: Tell us again of the wooden horse;
              give us an ageless rhyme
              of heroes and battles, of meddling gods,
              and a city lost to time.

Cassandra

But this is evil, see!
Now once again the pain of grim, true prophecy
Shivers my whirling brain in a storm of things foreseen.
—**Aeschylus**, *Agamemnon*, 480 B.C.

Cassandra's Chant

I,
Cassandra, see it all—
the horse's belly swarming with Greeks,
our city's fall
in fire and blood,
a bitter end—
before it happens,
again and again.
This hated gift—my second sight—
brings images struck with Apollo's light
unbidden to my inner eye;
my mind, the prison where I must watch
my people die
before it happens,
again and again,
in fire and blood—
a bitter end.

What good are the oracles to men?
Words, more words, and the hurt comes
upon us . . . terror and the truth.
—**Aeschylus,** *Agamemnon,* 480 B.C.

Trojan Chant I

O daughter of Priam,
princess,
priestess,
farsighted sister of Hector,
release us
from ominous portents,
your visions of doom,
prophetess,
pythoness,
voice of the tomb!
Be silent,
Cassandra;
your prophesies grieve us.
Calamity chanter,
dark oracle—
leave us!

O daughter of Priam,
princess,
priestess,
farsighted sister of Hector,
release us
from ominous portents,
your visions of doom,
prophetess,
pythoness,
voice of the tomb!

Paris . . .
Eloped with a young bride, seduced her, stole her,
Which opened a long war against the Trojans.
A thousand ships and every living Greek
And their allies set sail.
—**Ovid,** *The Metamorphoses*, Book XII, 8 A.D.

Aphrodite Explains Everything

Truly, I tell you, the Trojans' fall
  had little to do with a wooden horse.
If my fellow Olympians hadn't conspired
  with mortals to turn aside love's true course,
    then true love would conquer, peace would reign,
    and Troy would be standing. Let me explain:
When Paris, the handsomest man in Troy,
  met Helen, the fairest woman in Greece,
they fell madly in love—what *else* could have happened?
  Sadly, she couldn't obtain her release
    from a marriage arranged by those heartless Fates;
    now Helen's the woman all Greece hates!
King Menelaus, her powerful husband,
  was ruler of Sparta, was a vengeful man
who called on his neighbors to help him recover
  his chattel—his wife. The bloodshed began.

Helen, who'd slipped through his fingertips—
    Helen, whose face launched a thousand ships
across the Aegean to high-walled Troy—
    was the innocent pawn in their ten-year war.
The conspirators—Hera, Athena, Poseidon—
    attacked and harassed me, because I swore
        to protect the doomed lovers—what *else* could I do?
        If not the goddess of love, then who?

It is the gods' relentlessness, the gods',
that overturns these riches, tumbles Troy
from its high pinnacle.
—**Virgil**, *The Aeneid*, Book II, 19 B.C.

The Apple of Discord I

Eris (Goddess of Discord) Speaks

Lofty Olympians
   like to exclude
lesser immortals
   who aren't imbued
with the kind of power
   they so admire.
Still, I'm a goddess,
   and I require
certain courtesies,
   a little care and concern,
but the gods are hardheaded;
   they never learn.
So I came, uninvited,
   to the sea queen's wedding
and threw a gold apple
   far out on the spreading,
goddess-strewn lawn.

Inscribed, "for the fairest,"
it caused a commotion—
   weren't they embarrassed
to squabble that way?
   Hera, Athena,
and vain Aphrodite,
   tugging and pulling—
what high and mighty
   hypocrites! They claim
I'm the foul one!
They think they can blame
   my wedding surprise
for the horrors at Troy,
   when *they* are the guilty ones—
they who destroy,
   who sacrifice heroes,
Earth's glorious sons,
   like bulls on an altar—
brave, innocent ones.

   To their lasting shame,
they let Troy burn.
   The gods are hardheaded;
      they never learn.

The Apple of Discord II

Hera Speaks

Sunlight revealed it, a gleam in the grass,
   a shimmering apple. I watched it pass
the immortal throng as it streaked my way,
   swift as Apollo's fiery ray,
guided, it seemed, by his golden hand—
   exactly as Eris, Night's daughter, planned.

That Aphrodite's a brazen one;
   before I could reach it, she'd already swung
her foot out in front of me, halting the course
   of Eris's apple, which struck with such force,
it injured her heel, and it served her right!
   She wasn't, however, the least contrite,
insisting, instead, the apple was hers.
   She argued with *me*, the Thunderer's
own wife—his queen! How could she dare?
   Her insolent manner was hard to bear.

Athena? She's homely; her eyes, stone gray.
   Why she decided to claim it that day
I cannot imagine, but claim it she did.
   What nonsense—the two of them fighting amid
the divine ones who toasted the wedding couple.
   I struggled in vain to resolve the trouble,
pleading with Zeus, though I knew he'd refuse—
   I'm still so upset he didn't choose
to judge us himself! The rest is known:
   how the kingdom of Troy was forced to atone
for the bargain struck by Aphrodite;
   how Paris abducted the wife of the mighty
Spartan king, incurring his wrath
   and the dreadfully bloody aftermath.
It's a comfort to know the right side won—
   no one can change what the Fates have spun.
A wrong was righted and justice served.
   Troy was punished as it deserved,
but what of the cost? So many died,
   as the priestess Cassandra prophesied.
No one is left now to call our names,
   no one to kindle our temple flames.
Troy is gone—a glorious dream,
   fading with time like the apple's gleam.

Now, Paris, if you vote in my favor,
you'll never lose a battle. You'll always be
victorious. I'll make you a conquering hero.
—**Lucian** (Athena speaking in *The Judgment of Paris*, Book XX: 11–14)

The Apple of Discord III

Athena Speaks

Why did I claim the prize?
   The "fairest" must be wise,
impartial, and just—not vain,
   like the others. I disdain
appearances. And fashion?
   Meaningless! My passion
is craftsmanship—useful arts.
   Mere artfulness rules their hearts.

Who is fairest, then?
   Aphrodite, beguiler of men,
who confuses wrong with right?
   Hera, blinded by spite?
Good judgment commences
   when wisdom rules the senses.
Therefore, the choice is clear;
   I wield a balanced spear.

When you get to Sparta, Helen will see you. The rest—to make her
fall in love and follow you home—will be up to me. . . . I promise
that I shall make Helen your wife.
—**Lucian** (Aphrodite speaking in *The Judgment of Paris*, Book XX: 15–16)

The Apple of Discord IV

Aphrodite Speaks

I alone had the right to claim it.
Ask anyone—Eris aimed it
straight *at* me when she rolled
that troublemaking ball of gold
across the crowded lawn.
It was irresistibly drawn
to my naked heel,
like a magnet to steel.

The impact raised a welt;
despite the throbbing pain, I felt
responsible—wasn't my duty
as goddess of love and beauty
to claim the fairest's rightful prize?
Could I afford to do otherwise?

Hera, of course, complained to Zeus,
who offered the same old tired excuse
(too busy) and sent us all to Troy.
It was Paris, that handsome shepherd boy,
who judged between us, sought me out,
and (as if there were ever any doubt)
gave *me* the apple—justice prevailed.
Athena stood scowling; Hera wailed.
I pity our bitter cow-eyed queen,
but I loathe that battle-ax, Athene—
too clever and *so* ill-bred.
Imagine her springing
from Zeus's head,
a nightmare come to life.
She stirred up *all* this strife!

The three goddesses came
to remote Ida, and to Paris, for him to judge
their loveliness, and beauty was the cause.
—**Euripides**, *Helen*, 412 B.C.

The Judgment of Paris

I was camped at the foot of Mount Ida,
    guarding my flocks of sheep,
turning my thoughts in the firelight,
    resisting the call to sleep,
when three resplendent figures
    appeared in a blinding vision—
goddesses. They commanded,
    "Paris, make the decision.

"Which of us will it be?
    Who shall be called the most beautiful?
Zeus, in his infinite wisdom,
    has deemed you his valued and dutiful
servant, the handsomest mortal,
    and, therefore, the only one qualified
to judge among the three of us."
    I clung to the stone-ringed fireside.

Paris

No words would come; no reply
 could rise from my tightening throat.
They assured me I wasn't in danger.
 However I'd cast my vote,
the three would accept my decision,
 returning the way they came.
Each of them offered me prizes:
 Queen Hera's was fortune and fame.
Athena would make me the victor
 in battle, a glorious life,
but I chose Aphrodite,
 who promised to give me a wife
beyond compare—a mortal
 whose beauty would rival my own.
My days as a shepherd were over,
 the seeds of destruction sown.

Troy, my beloved homeland,
 perished because I believed
the goddesses' reassurances.
 In the end, I was deceived,
for the gods can never be trusted.
 Olympian hearts are cruel;
we are their servants and playthings;
 vengeance, their only rule.

Keep her far off, the Greek heifer is coming.
Sink that unclean ship while there is time;
It is heavy with the weight of Trojan blood.
—**Ovid,** *Heroides,* Book V: 1 2–1 0 B.C.

Cassandra and Paris

CASSANDRA: Brother, you stand before me,
    expecting a welcome home,
your arms enfolding a woman
    as pale as the ocean foam,
the wife of Menelaus—
    you've made this king our foe!
She's beautiful, your Helen,
    but dangerous. Let her go
before she sets a foot
    on innocent Trojan sod.
Her presence dooms us all—
    I swear, by the shining god
Apollo who grants me vision,
    she brings us a gruesome fate.
Brother, you must return her;
    soon it will be too late.

PARIS: Calm yourself, Cassandra;
    people will think you mad.
Have you forgotten your manners?
    Give me your hand. Be glad
for the safe return of your kinsman;
    welcome my bride-to-be.
Sing your doom song elsewhere;
    it makes no sense to me.

CASSANDRA: Send her back to Sparta—
    if you don't, it is you who are mad!
Do you wish to see our city
    overrun by the armor-clad
allies of Menelaus,
    the husband she left behind?

You believe I've lost my senses—
   how can you be so blind?
Can't you see the Greek ships
   moored in the harbor there?
Don't you hear their war cry,
   the chanting of battle prayer?
Listen—war god Ares
   knocks at the Trojan gate.
Brother, I beg you, return her.
   Soon it will be too late.

Rumor told news of the Greek ships advancing,
Of their armed forces eager for the battle;
Therefore the invasion came without surprise.
The Trojans were prepared to meet the invaders,
To resist a beachhead made upon their shores. . . .
—**Ovid,** *The Metamorphoses,* Book XII

Greek Warrior's Chant

Pallas
Athena,
ally,
friend—
stand
at my side!
Help me
defend
family,
home,
my gods,
my ways.
Turn your
terrible
steel-eyed
gaze
upon my
enemy.

Guide
my
spear.
Shield
my
back.
KILL
MY
FEAR.
Keep
me
strong
to my
fated
end,
Pallas
Athena,
ally—
friend!

> Sing, goddess, of the anger of Peleus' son Achilles
> and its devastation, which put pains thousandfold upon the Greeks. . . .
> —**Homer,** *The Iliad*, Book I, 800 B.C.

Athena's Complaint

Make no mistake—
  I side with the Greeks,
but their leader's a fool.
  Agamemnon seeks
to profit from war
  at his soldier's expense.
He takes what he pleases—
  his crown, his defense.

That dog-eyed coward,
  he's done it again—
dishonored and bullied
  the bravest of men,
Achilles, bold son
  of the sea goddess Thetis.
Without him, the Trojans
  are bound to defeat us.

Look at him crouching
   alone on the shore—
Achilles, stripped
   of his spoils of war,
a gift he earned,
   the debt still owed.
His anger's just;
   his armor, stowed.

&#x1FnbspFE;

> But Achilles
> weeping went and sat in sorrow apart from his companions
> beside the beach of the grey sea looking in the infinite water.
> Many times stretching forth his hands he called on his mother.
> —**Homer,** *The Iliad*, Book I

Achilles' Plea

Mother, make him pay—
how can I bear this shame?
He took it all away,
my prize, my pride, my honored name.
How can I bear this shame?
Goddess, defend your son—
my prize, my pride, my honored name—
you are the only one.
Goddess, defend your son—
he took it all away!
You are the only one,
Mother. Make him pay.

Zeus

Nor did Thetis forget the entreaties
of her son [Achilles], but she emerged from the waves early
in the morning and went up to the tall sky and Olympus.
—**Homer,** *The Iliad,* Book I

Thetis

At the Feet of Zeus

THETIS: Zeus, I must ask a favor.
  You've seen how Achilles stays
by his ships and forsakes the battle
  because of the shameful ways
he was treated by Agamemnon,
  who has taken his rightful prize,
the slave-girl Achilles loves—
  the one with the beautiful eyes.
I beg you, strengthen the Trojans
  until the thief returns
what he stole—until this king,
  Agamemnon of Argos, learns
to respect my son, his equal!
  Punish his cruelty;
restore Achilles' honor.
  Give Troy the victory.

ZEUS: Ask me for anything else,
               but please don't ask for this—
           go, before Hera suspects
               something's amiss!

THETIS: I, daughter of Nereus—
               you mean to dishonor me?
           You'd offend my ancient father
               by sending me back to the sea?

ZEUS: Thetis, the matter's disastrous—
               you'll set me against my wife.

THETIS: Hera's against you already;
               the two of you live in strife.

ZEUS: Now—before she sees us.
               I'll see what I can do.
           You know the Fates will have their way
               before this war is through.

Alas, alas for the wretchedness of my ill-starred life;
this pain flooding the song of sorrow is mine alone. . . .
—**Aeschylus** (Cassandra in *Agamemnon*)

King Agamemnon and His Servant

Beneath the Trojan Wall

KING:
> Who stands there, on the wall—
> that woman—alone in the gloom,
> with her robes and hair undone,
> chanting those songs of doom?

SERVANT:
> *Cassandra, my king, the priestess*
> *great Apollo, the sun god, wooed.*
> *The story goes, she refused him.*
> *No man or god ever subdued*
> *the heart she guards too well.*
> *Listen—she prophesies*
> *we'll burn their citadel!*

KING:
> If it comes to pass,
> let this be known:
> Of the Trojan spoils,
> she is marked my own.

No longer shall my prophecies like some young girl
new-married glance from under veils, but bright and strong
as winds blow into morning and the sun's uprise
shall wax along the swell like some great wave, to burst
at last upon the shining of this agony.
—**Aeschylus** (Cassandra in *Agamemnon*)

Cassandra

At the Trojan Wall

I sense him in the darkness,
feel his greedy stare.
Agamemnon,
Agamemnon,
his name assaults the air.
This Greek! This hateful sound!
I shudder to repeat it.
Agamemnon,
Agamemnon,
when all Troy lies defeated,
you plan to claim me as your prize—
Apollo's priestess—
is it wise?

I know the future
far too well;
I've watched you burn our citadel,
seen your soldiers kill and maim,
heard them call your ugly name,
"Agamemnon!"
"Agamemnon!"
I promise you, Agamemnon,
I'll feed no fool's obsession.
I'll be no
king's
possession.

But Poseidon who circles the earth and shakes it
rose up out of the deep water to stir on the Greeks. . . .
—**Homer,** *The Iliad,* Book XIII

Iris, Goddess of the Rainbow, Delivers a Message to Poseidon

IRIS: Sea King, I come with a message
           from your brother, almighty Zeus.
        He says you must quit the fighting;
           he'll listen to no excuse.
        He sees through your many disguises
           and watches you out on the field,
        inciting the Greeks to battle
           behind your invincible shield.
        Return with me now to Olympus,
           or stay in your turbulent sea.
        If you don't, he's prepared to declare you
           the Thunderer's enemy.
        Poseidon, your brother is powerful;
           to fight him would be a mistake.
        He waits on his throne for an answer.
           Take care what decision you make.

POSEIDON: This time he goes too far!
    I, his equal in rank,
wander the Earth as I please!
    Tell him I never shrank
from a fight since the world began—
    he thinks I'd avoid one now?
No! But I'll make him a bargain,
    backed by my solemn vow:
I'll return to my home in the sea
    as long as the Thunderer stays
far away from the walls of Troy.
    His meddling only delays
what the Fates have already decreed—
    or doesn't he know the story?
His Trojans are marked for defeat;
    these Greeks, for eternal glory.

So he spoke . . . and about them
the ships echoed terribly to the roaring of Greeks
as they cried out applause to the word of godlike Odysseus.
—Homer, *The Iliad*, Book II

Greek Hero Odysseus Addresses His Men

GREEK MEN: Odysseus—how much longer
    must we sharpen our death-dulled spears?
Our bodies are battered and weary.
    We've suffered these ten long years
without seeing our families and homelands.
    Why did we join in this endless strife?
For the honor of Menelaus?
    We're fools—chasing Helen, his faithless wife!
Our ships are in need of repairing.
    Cables are broken; the wood rots away.
Before they all sink, we should fix them—
    leave this forsaken, blood-drenched bay!

ODYSSEUS: *Friends, do you mean to betray*
    the solemn vow you made,
to fight until every Trojan
    had fallen beneath your blade?

When did you lose your faith
    in the voices of prophecy?
You've forgotten the oracle, Calchas,
    at Aulis, beside the sea,
when he spoke to our camp at the harbor
    where a thousand ships were moored?
After the offering of milk
    and the bowls of blood were poured,
a sign from our gods appeared—
    a snake—by the altar stone.
It coiled round a nearby tree
    where a mother bird had flown.
As she fluttered about its head,
    desperate to save her young,
the serpent discovered her nest
    and devoured them, one by one,

then struck the mother down,
　　squeezing away her life.
Remember the seer's chant?
　　"Nine years of bitter strife!
This is the number set:
　　for every bird, one year
of battle, blood, and death.
　　Greeks, you must persevere,
for in the tenth—success:
　　Troy's citadel will fall."
Finally our fate is upon us!
　　Now you decide to haul
our stranded ships to the ocean,
　　unfurling the sails in flight?
Do as your consciences bid you;
　　mine tells me, "Keep up the fight."

But Hector went away to the house of Paris. . . .
He found the man in his chamber busy with his splendid armor . . .
while Helen of Argos was sitting among her attendant women
directing the magnificent work done by her handmaidens.
—**Homer**, *The Iliad*, Book VI

Hector and Paris

The Hero of Troy Confronts His Brother

HECTOR: Paris, our people are dying,
     defending the city wall.
Strange man, do you think it fair,
     lying idle inside your hall?
For your sake, this bloodshed continues—
     rise up now! Prepare to fight!
We can't keep the city from burning
     by avoiding the battle site.

PARIS: *Brother, you've scolded me rightly.*
     Only listen; let me explain.
I'm fighting a war with Sorrow,
     and it forced me to leave the plain.
Ask Helen—she sees how I grieve
     for our comrades who breathe no more—

HECTOR: If the earth opened wide right beneath you
and swallowed you whole, I would pour
a jarful of wine in thanksgiving.
Rise up now! Prepare to fight
or I swear I'll drag you, naked,
by your feet to the battle site!

> Poor Andromache! Why does your heart sorrow so much for me?
> No man is going to hurl me to Hades, unless it is fated,
> But as for fate, I think that no man yet has escaped it. . . .
> —**Homer** (Hector speaking to his wife in *The Iliad*, Book VI)

Andromache's Message

Sent to the Battlefront

Hector, beloved,
                              last night in the stillness
I sought you. Fleeing our bedchamber,
sleepless, I climbed the high ramparts, unnoticed
        by sentries who scoured the black night,
their senses straining only for enemies.
        As the lone shepherd comforts himself
by gazing in silence at numberless stars,
        so I contemplated the watch fires
set by Trojans, flickering in the clear air.
        Thousands I saw there on the dark plain,
bright as stars, and I knew that beside each one
        sat fifty brave men. You, my husband,
wrapped in the blanket I wove, sat among them.
        Come home to me.
                              Your Andromache

Hector, when he saw high-hearted Patroklos
trying to get away, saw how he was wounded
by the sharp javelin, came close against him across the ranks,
and with the spear stabbed him in the belly and drove
the bronze clean through.
—**Homer,** *The Iliad,* Book XVI

Achilles' Wrath

Patroklos, my friend, is dead;
in anger, I cannot mourn.
This fire burns in my head,
this flame of hatred born
in anger—I cannot mourn
as long as Hector lives!
This flame of hatred born
pure, inviolate, gives—
as long as Hector lives—
cold purpose to my cause—
pure, inviolate—gives—
a substance without flaws—
cold purpose to my cause—
Patroklos—my friend, is dead!
A substance without flaws—
this fire—burns in my head!
Patroklos, my friend, is dead!

Achilles

> So the men of both sides in a cramped space tugged at the body
> [of Patroklos] in both directions; and the hearts of the Trojans
> were hopeful to drag him [Patroklos] away to Troy, and those of the
> Greeks to get him back to the hollow ships, and about him a savage
> struggle arose.
> —**Homer,** *The Iliad,* Book XVII

King Priam's Messenger

My king, I come from the battle,
    where I witnessed a terrible sight.
I swear by the gods, what I tell you
    is true. Troy was winning the fight;
we were hauling Patroklos's body
    back to our camp as a prize,
when Achilles appeared by the black ships.
    He seemed like a god in disguise,
towering above his companions,
    roaring his dead friend's name,
with a strange light burning above him—
    he looked like his hair was aflame.

No armor protected his body,
    no weaponry flashed in his hand,
but he struck blind fear in our warriors,
    who dropped his Patroklos and ran.
Hector stood over the body,
    shouting until they returned.

Achilles continued to bellow;
   the flames on his head still burned.
Three times we reclaimed the prize,
   attacking with all our might.
Three times, as Achilles shouted,
   our horses stampeded in fright.

Trojan soldiers were thrown in confusion;
   one fell on his own sharp spear.
So many were trampled by horses;
   others were able to steer
their chariots back to the campsite.
   Faced with our sudden defeat,
we prepared to return to the city,
   but Hector refused to retreat.
He sent me to tell you what happened.
   Twelve of our bravest were lost.
I'm afraid he will stand his ground there,
   no matter how great the cost.

Hector

Then [Zeus] the Father balanced his golden scales, and in them
he set two fateful portions of death, which lays men prostrate,
one for Achilles, and one for Hector, breaker of horses,
and balanced it in the middle, and Hector's death-day was heavier. . . .
—**Homer,** *The Iliad*, Book XXII

Hector and Achilles

HECTOR: Son of Thetis—Troy's affliction—
at last, Achilles, we meet.
Will you forfeit your life at this moment
or strip me of mine? If defeat
is destined for you, then I swear
—no oath have I ever forsaken—
I'll give back your corpse to the Greeks
as soon as your new armor's taken.

ACHILLES: *No high sounding words—no agreements!*
Die like the dog you are!
Let the vultures feed on your carcass;
your family can mourn from afar
The gods have abandoned you, Hector.
Athena's delivered you here—
see her, disguised as your brother?
Now—twist beneath my spear!

HECTOR: The gods command it—*all* bodies
must burn on the funeral heap.

ACHILLES: *Zeus himself couldn't move me;*
this hatred runs too deep.

Andromache at the Wall

Hector, how dare you—your son, just a baby?
Did you not think of us? Did you not hear,
as the others retreated, your heart when it whispered,
You have a wife now; you have a child,
or was it silent, my stubborn defender,
duty bound, driven to glory or death?
Could honor—the prize for such bitter courage—
be cupped, like your chin, in my hand? Can I—
obedient soul—ever nuzzle your cheek,
tousle the curls on that proud, hard head,
now bloodied? What has our goodness begotten—
this body tossing behind a Greek chariot?
What has our goodness begotten—your body—
that proud head pounding—my heart—on the hard ground—
our son, just a baby? Hector. How dare you.

Paris' Chant

Lord Apollo, guide my arrow;
help avenge our fallen hero,

Hector. Grant a steady hand.
Spread my fame throughout the land:

"Paris, great Achilles' slayer."
Lord Apollo, hear my prayer.

Take this poisoned point of steel;
drive it through Achilles' heel.

Show no mercy. Make his mother
mourn, as mine does, for my brother.

Help avenge our fallen hero;
lord Apollo, guide my arrow.

And the goddesses gathered about [Thetis] . . .
all who along the depths of the sea were daughters of Nereus.
—**Homer,** *The Iliad,* Book XVIII

Thetis' Song

Daughters of Nereus, rise from the sea.
Kalianassa, come to me;
golden-haired Doris, gentle Doto,
Panope, Thaleia, silver-limbed Proto,
abandon the depths, our ancient home.
Head for its trembling, sunlit dome
and high-walled Troy, that town I dread.
Swim with me, sisters; my son lies dead,
my only son. I failed to keep him
safe, though I tried. Before they heap him
high on a driftwood funeral pyre,
before he burns in the sacred fire—
swiftly, sisters, I must see him.
His fate was set; I couldn't free him.
How could Paris, that cowardly charmer,
pierce my Achilles' immortal armor?
Sweet Galateia, my Klymene, come;
beat the bright waves, our sorrowful drum.
Swim with me, sisters; rise from the sea,
daughters of Nereus. Come to me.

The fear, the horror of the Trojan people,
    The pride of every Greek. . . .
The great Achilles came at last to ashes,
    A scant handful in a polished urn.
His splendor lives; it fills the rounded world. . . .
    His shield still goes to war against the world,
    And in his name all weapons go to war.
       —**Ovid,** *The Metamorphoses,* Book XII

Prayer of Odysseus

Give me the words, Athena,
   to make Greek courage flow,
some hopeful sign or vision;
   show me the way to go.
We thought the worst was over—
   victory seemed at hand.
Goddess, what do I tell them,
   these men in my command,
who sailed with me from Ithaca,
   who've fought and killed and bled?
What will stir their valor,
   with great Achilles dead?

Once, I plowed and planted.
   Reluctantly, I agreed
to fight here, in your service,
   to follow wherever you'd lead.

My son was just a boy then;
   now he's nearly grown.
Like a widow, my Penelope
   raises him all alone.
With no one to teach him war craft,
   how will he keep our lands
from falling to foreign invaders,
   safe from pirate bands?

Goddess, you know I'm no coward.
   I've never avoided a fight,
but battle scarred and homesick,
   I suffer my countrymen's plight.
Give me your answer, Athena;
   help me understand.
Grant us strength to continue
   fighting hand to hand,
if fight we must. But tell me;
   with thousands of comrades slain,
why should more Greek corpses
   litter this bloody plain?

Athena Speaks to Odysseus

I stand by you still, Odysseus.
　Patience; the end is near.
Inspire the Greeks to greatness;
　persuade the mutineer
to honor his vow of duty.
　Encourage your men to excel
with artful phrases, spoken
　in the voice you employ so well.

Summon our friend Diomedes;
　there is something you both must do.
Under the cover of darkness,
　slip past the watchful crew
of Trojans lining the ramparts,
　and climb to my temple. There,
you will find an oaken likeness—
　a sculpture beyond compare.

Take my Palladium down
  from the wall of the Trojan shrine.
Return with it to your campsite;
  let it be a victory sign,
for I stand by you still, Odysseus.
  My image will ease their fear,
inspiring the Greeks to greatness.
  Patience; the end is near.

Athena

Epitaph

Here lie the bones of bold Hector and Paris,
sons of King Priam,
dark death uniting two who in life were divided.

Hector, respected commander of Trojans,
courageous in battle,
devoted father, faithful to dark-eyed Andromache,
famed as the greatest of Troy's tested heroes,
was tricked by Athena,
cut down through treachery, struck by Achilles' spear.

Paris, praised for his beauty, was banished at birth
by his father,
royal Priam, fearing his wife's dream of prophesy:
"Troy shall be burned by the torch in my womb!"
He lived as a shepherd,
returned to Troy, carrying Helen of Sparta,
gift of the goddess, the flame in his heart that would
kindle destruction.
He died for love, killed by Greek archer Philoctetes.

> Come to another part of the story, sing us
> the wooden horse, which Epeios made with Athene helping,
> the stratagem great Odysseus filled once with men. . . .
> —Homer, *The Odyssey,* Book VIII

Epeios, the Builder

Every endeavor begins with a singular vision.
What came in the night to Odysseus, cloaked in a dream,
unveiled itself by day. His deadly scheme
required my skills: mathematical precision,
a discerning eye, artistic intuition,
and knowledge of the builder's special rules,
the ways to draw a plan, to use the tools.
I've learned the column's secret, the way the beam
and post are joined to bear a heavy load,
how stones within a wall must be aligned.
Ten years I've trod an unfamiliar road,
this bloody path, and yet, somehow, I'll find
my way. Whatever depths the spirit plumbs—
always, out of chaos order comes.

The captains of the Greeks,
now weak with war and beaten back by fate,
and with so many years gone by,
are able to construct, through the divine
art of Athena, a mountainous horse.
—**Virgil**, *The Aeneid*, Book II

Trojan Voices
Overheard at the Wall

What are they building?
    What *is* that thing?
A battering ram?
    Scaffolding?
Could it breach our wall?
    What have they done?
Cleared the whole forest.
    Look, they've begun
to lash those fresh-cut planks—
    white pine—
in giant circles.
    Strange design.

That dog, Odysseus—
     it's his?
Of course.
     That piece over there—
the head of a

   horse?

A gift for the gods?
     A peace offering.
What are they building?
     What is that thing?

They weave its ribs with sawed-off beams of fir,
pretending that it is an offering
for safe return. At least, that is their story.
—Virgil, *The Aeneid*, Book II

Greek Voices
Overheard Outside the Camp

What are we building?
    What *is* this thing?
A trap, they say, for capturing—
    the citadel?
It can't be done.
    They'll pack us inside it?
Not me.
    You'll run?
The Trojans aren't stupid.
    We don't have a prayer.
They'll pack us inside it?
    Pitch black.
No air.

That dog, Odysseus—
it's his?
　　Of course.
Who else could convince us
　　to build this—

　　　　horse?

They'll pack us inside it—
　　quit grumbling!
What are we building?
　　What *is* this thing?

Then in the dark sides of the horse they hide
men chosen from the sturdiest among them;
they stuff their soldiers in its belly, deep
in the vast cavern: Greeks armed to the teeth.
—**Virgil,** *The Aeneid,* Book II

Final Instructions of Odysseus

Diomedes, raise your torch—
  comrades, look inside.
Behold and marvel. Memorize
  each plank. This place we hide
will bring about our victory
  and seal the Trojans' doom
or cause our deaths. Mark it well;
  this horse may be your tomb.
You captains—Thoas, Acamus—
  take your men down first.
Pyrrhus, pass the wineskins out;
  we'll need to quench our thirst.
Watch your rations; make them last
  all day and through this night.
Keep helmets on, swords at hand,
  in case we need to fight.

Odysseus

If they suspect our hiding place,
    they'll flush us out with fire.
Aias—use your mighty ax
    to free us, if this pyre
goes up. With luck, we'll see our homes
    again. We'll hold our wives.
Goddess, in your gracious hands
    we place our hopes, our lives.
Hail, Athena! We praise your gifts—
    skill and discipline.
Bow your heads, men. Give her thanks
    before we're shut within.
She just might save our skin.

> And all of Troy is free
> of long lament. The gates are opened wide.
> —**Virgil,** *The Aeneid,* Book II

King Priam's Messenger II

My king, the Greeks are gone.
Their camp's unoccupied;
their hollow ships, withdrawn,

unnoticed, on the tide.
I tell you, sire, it's done—
Greek ships have all withdrawn!

A shout rang out at dawn;
the gates are opened wide.
My king, the Greeks are gone—

come see—our people don
bright robes and roam outside.
Greek ships have all withdrawn—

I tell you, sire, we've won!
This joy is justified,
my king. The Greeks are gone,
their hollow ships withdrawn!

> Gladly we go to see the [Greek] camp,
> deserted places, the abandoned sands . . .
> here fierce Achilles once had pitched his tent;
> and here their ships were anchored, here they fought.
> —**Virgil,** *The Aeneid,* Book II

King Priam

Ten years ago I stood upon
    this barren shore beside
my wife and watched my wayward son
    returning with his bride.
The evils Paris brought with him
    can never be undone.
Our silver beach ran black with blood.
    No potent shaft of sun
can bleach it clean; no blast of wind
    can banish it; no rain
or cleansing lash of tidal wave
    can wash away the stain.

Twenty years ago my sons
    hurled rocks into the sea
and charged the surf, imploring me
    to join their revelry.

I watched them play from this same spot,
    a memory I cherish.
Back then, I never thought I'd reach
    this age; I knew I'd perish
long before those sturdy boys.
    Then came the Greek attack.
Now nothing gods or men can do
    will bring my children back.

Two months ago I stood right here,
    inside the tent of one
I hated; on my knees, I kissed
    the hand that killed my son,
my Hector, shining light of Troy.
    I begged to be allowed
to bring his battered body home.
    They wrapped him in a shroud.
Brutal Achilles lifted him
    above the wagon's wheel
and set him on its wooden bed,
    then offered me a meal.

He talked in halting, quiet tones,
 of life and death. We wept,
remembering the ones we'd lost,
 before we finally slept.
We never spoke another word;
 I left before the dawn.
Within a week Achilles died.
 Today Greek tents are gone
and Troy rejoices. Still, I can't
 forget his stricken face,
the way he held my lifeless son,
 the horror of this place.

Some wonder at the deadly gift . . .
marveling at the horse's bulk.
Thymoetes was the first of us to urge
that it be brought within the walls and set
inside the citadel.
—Virgil, *The Aeneid*, Book II

A Trojan's Plea

What are we waiting for?
Haul the horse in—
what do we care
of its origin?
It's ours to claim;
the Greeks have gone,
scuttling home
to their scheming spawn.
Wind it with garlands
our women plait;
parade through the city—
celebrate!
So many years—
at last, we win.
What are we waiting for?
Haul the horse in!

Those with sounder judgment counsel us
to cast the Greek device into the sea,
or to set fire to this suspicious gift.
The lead is taken by Laocoön.
He hurries from the citadel's high point
excitedly; and with a mob around him
from far off he calls out. . . .
—**Virgil**, *The Aeneid*, Book II

Laocoön, Priest of Poseidon, Speaks

Trojans, have you lost your minds?
    What wild insanity,
to drag this horse inside our walls—
    you'd trust our enemy?
What makes you all so certain
    the Greeks are gone for good?
I promise you, there's treachery
    shut within this wood.
Ask yourselves, is this the way
    that fiend Odysseus acts?
Take his gift; you'll pay the price,
    but when his crew attacks,
don't say I didn't warn you.
    Don't look for Laocoön
to help you when Greek soldiers torch
    your houses—I'll be gone.

And as [Laocoön] . . . spoke he hurled his massive shaft
with heavy force against the side, against
the rounded, jointed belly of the beast.
It quivered when it struck the hollow cavern,
which groaned and echoed.
—**Virgil**, *The Aeneid*, Book II

Inside the Wooden Horse

A netted fish
my water gone
must suck what little air's
remaining drenched
in sweat and darkness
formulating prayers
inside my head
no god can hear
no power from on high
will reach inside
this stinking hole
lift me to the sky
god lift me sky god
let me breathe
hold me in the light
lift me hold me
help me please
make it through this night

Wooden Horse

please make it stop
this din of death
clanging in my ear
inside my head
this din of death
I don't want to hear
please make it stop
don't let me feel
what echoes in my brain
pulsing to each swallowed moan
wet murmurings of pain
god help me sky god—
can't you hear?
Stop this awful flood!
The warmth I feel
beneath my heart, please,
let it not be blood.

Meanwhile with many shouts some [Trojan] shepherds
were dragging to the king a youth they had found.
His hands were bound behind his back. . . .
From every side the youth of Troy rush out,
all swarming in their eagerness to see him,
contending in their taunts against the captive.
Now listen to the treachery of the Greeks
and learn from one the wickedness of all.
—**Virgil**, *The Aeneid*, Book II

Sinon's Trickery

Great Priam, before you sentence me to die,
before more blood is spilled, please, let me speak.
Your people think I came here as a spy.

In truth, I can't deny I'm born a Greek,
but I am innocent of any crime.
Betrayed by my own kind, I'm forced to seek

your mercy. Lord, I beg you, give me time
to tell of my ordeal, how I was made
a sacrifice—stripped bare and forced to climb

the altar steps. Before the high priest's blade
could end my life, the ground began to shake.
I ran, and in the rushes of a glade,

hid myself for days. Poseidon's quake
saved my life, but soon, a renegade,
I feared Greek wrath. My future still at stake,

I formed a plan, intending to persuade
them I had leaped into the surf and drowned.
It worked; I watched them leave, the black ships fade

into the dark horizon, homeward bound.
The Greeks would kill their own for nothing more
than favorable winds—a truth I've found

too hard to bear. I fought their bloody war;
they show their thanks by trying to butcher me?
My anger boils; hate seeps from every pore,

extinguishing all flames of loyalty.
I'm sure I speak to one who understands.
There's so much more to tell you. Set me free.

I beg you, lord, unbind my bleeding hands;
these cursed ropes will cut me to the bone.
You know Athena's awesome power demands

respect—a fact we Greeks should well have known.
By stealing the Palladium, we brought
her fury down; we needed to atone.

We built this work of art, superbly wrought,
to serve as payment for our sacrilege.
It had to be enormous, so we thought,

for if you Trojans found a way to wedge
the horse's bulk between your city's gates,
you'd gain Athena's might and patronage.

The truth is finally out. Perhaps the Fates
meant to save you from Athena's ire.
Mark my words, whoever advocates

destruction of this present plays with fire;
but if you get it past the city wall,
Troy's future is secure, I promise, sire.

Have mercy, gracious King. Let Sinon call
your land his home, the Trojan people, friend.
I've tried to be of service, after all.

My story's done; now *you* must tell its end.

Such was the art of perjured Sinon . . .
insidious, we trusted what he told
so we were taken in by snares, forced tears—
yes, we, whom neither Diomedes nor
Achilles of Larissa could defeat,
nor ten long years, a thousand-galleyed fleet.
—**Virgil**, *The Aeneid*, Book II

Trojan Chant I

Unbind the boy—
set Sinon free.
Peace for Troy!
Amnesty!
No more bloodshed,
no more tears;
we must put
away our fears.
Hear us, Trojans—
help us seek
mercy for this
brave young Greek!
Amnesty!
Peace for Troy!
Set Sinon free—
unbind the boy.

The doubting crowd is split into two factions.
—**Virgil**, *The Aeneid*, Book II

Trojan Chant II

Don't believe
this lying Greek.
Death to Sinon!
Make him seek
mercy in the
underworld;
send him there
on Trojan-hurled
axes, knives,
ash-wood spears!
Let him drown
in phony tears!
Don't believe
a word he speaks—
Sinon's lying.
Death to Greeks!

Now yet another and more dreadful omen
is thrust at us, bewilders our blind hearts.
Laocoön, by lot named priest of Neptune,
was sacrificing then a giant bull
upon the customary altars, when
two snakes with endless coils from Tenedos
strike out across the tranquil deep (I shudder
to tell what happened). . . .
—Virgil, *The Aeneid*, Book II

King Priam's Messenger III

What I'm about to tell you, sire,
   I shudder to repeat.
Laocoön had sacrificed a bull;
   the butchered meat
was waiting on the altar stone.
   His sons were at his side
assisting with the rituals,
   when two assassin-eyed
snakes with endless winding coils
   swept across the sea,
huge heads erect above the waves,
   approaching noiselessly,

bloodred crests that flapped and swayed
   like banners on the breeze.
What happened next, I tell you, sire,
   caused every heart to freeze.
These creatures, swift and purposeful,
   slithered up the shore
and headed straight for Laocoön,
   whose back was turned. Before
our shouts of warning reached his ears,
   the monsters' coils were wound
so tightly round his struggling boys,
   they were lifted off the ground.

Their father, drenched in blood and venom,
  fought ferociously
to save them, ripping at the coils,
  trying to wrest them free.
He bellowed like a wounded bull,
  stabbing with his knife,
but, wrapped around his neck, those serpents
  squeezed away his life,
then sank their fangs repeatedly
  in tangled, lifeless limbs,
feasting with their vicious jaws.
  Poseidon's altar brims
with burning venom, filth, and gore,
  their evil-smelling slime.
Sated, they uncoiled themselves.
  We saw the creatures climb
Athena's temple steps. Inside
  her colonnaded shrine,
they sleep behind her altar stone.
  This horrifying sign
stirs our people's passions, sire.
  The mob no longer waits;
the horse now stands on sliding wheels;
  they're tearing down the gates.

> . . . and unwed girls surround it, singing
> their sacred chants, so glad to touch the cable.
> The horse glides, menacing, advancing toward
> the center of the city. . . .
> Even then can Cassandra chant of what will come
> with lips the gods had doomed to disbelief.
> —**Virgil,** *The Aeneid,* Book II

Cassandra's Lament

Look at them,
linking arms,
girls I know by name,
dancing
in their circle,
my childhood friends.
What came—
impenetrably—
between us?
When did the curtain fall,
this crystalline awareness
descending
like a wall?

One side,
the world I love;
the other, only me.
I've tried;
I cannot reach them,
my friends,
my family.
No one seems to hear.
When did the curtain fall?
What can I do
but watch now
behind this crystal wall?

> Heedless, blinded by frenzy,
> we press right on and set the inauspicious
> monster inside the sacred fortress. . . .
> Helpless, we crown the altars of the gods
> with festive branches all about the city.
> —**Virgil**, *The Aeneid*, Book II

Trojan Festival Song

Wind our way with fragrant garlands.
  Weave a path to follow:
healing herbs for Artemis;
  laurel for Apollo;

stalks of grain for Demeter
  and pale Persephone;
cuttings from Athena's grove,
  her silver olive tree;

with shoots of anise, violets,
  and mountain hyacinth
to decorate each pillared shrine,
  from pedestal to plinth.

Hermes favors golden rushes
   starred with lotus flowers;
Dionysus, tendriled grape
   culled from sacred bowers.

A wreath of oak shall crown the head
   of mighty Zeus, but green
branches from a supple willow
   please his gracious queen.

To honor lord Poseidon, gather
   sea-swept limbs of pine;
for Aphrodite, pomegranate
   bound in braided vine;

healing herbs for Artemis,
   laurel for Apollo.
Wind our way with fragrant garlands;
   weave a path to follow.

Meanwhile, the heavens wheel, night hurries from
Ocean and clothes within its giant shadow
the earth, the sky, and the snares of Myrmedons.
—**Virgil,** *The Aeneid*, Book II

The Sentinel on the Trojan Wall

Dark hides
the empty plain;
no watch fires needed now.
Earth, sea, and shrouded sky are one
tonight,

seamless;
no moon, no stars,
no flames to pierce this cloak
of silken peace, first peace in ten
hard years.

The silent Trojans lie within their city,
as sleep embraces their exhausted bodies.
—**Virgil,** *The Aeneid,* Book II

Trojan Lullaby

Ride the wooden horse, my love,
   ride it off to bed.
Dream of pinewood dressed in garlands;
   rest your sleepy head.

Father's home; the war is over;
   all our troubles cease.
Ride the wooden horse, my love,
   through fields of dreamless peace.

Within my sleep,
before my eyes there seemed to stand, in tears and sorrow,
Hector as he once was. . . . He wastes no time on useless questions—
but drawing heavy sighs from deep within . . . he cries.
—**Virgil**, *The Aeneid*, Book II

Hector Speaks to Aeneas in a Dream

Goddess-born Aeneas, friend,
   rise now—leave your bed.
Our enemy swarms the city;
   our king's already dead.
Achilles' furious son
   dragged Priam by his hair
to the palace's marble altar
   and slaughtered the old man there.
Hecuba—poor mother—
   huddles near him still,
wailing my father's name,
   watching Pyrrhus spill
her children's blood; my brothers
   are falling, one by one.
Andromache's held captive;
   they've tossed my infant son

like rubbish from the ramparts.
　　Dead fathers can't defend
their loved ones from the living.
　　It's finished now, my friend.
No man or god can stop it—
　　promise me you'll leave.
Seek out Priam's altar;
　　there you must retrieve
my family's holy relics.
　　When you cross the sea,
take these icons with you—
　　do this thing for me.
A new land is waiting,
　　Aeneas. You'll survive.
Remember Troy the way it was.
　　Keep its name alive.

[Helen,] the common
Fury of Troy and of her homeland, she
had hid herself; she crouched, a hated thing . . .
anger spurs me to avenge my falling land.
—**Virgil** (Aeneas speaking in *The Aeneid of Virgil*, Book II)

Aeneas to Helen in the Ruins of Troy

Woman, look around you.
  Before you taste my blade,
drink your fill of bloody scenes.
  This wicked game you've played
cost too much—look around!
  Don't turn those eyes on me.
Drink your fill of bloody scenes—
  last you'll ever see.

Aphrodite

And carried off by my mad mind, I was
still blurting out these words when, with such brightness
as I had never seen, my gracious mother [Aphrodite]
stood there before me . . . and while she caught and held my right hand fast,
she spoke these words to me with her rose lips.
—**Virgil,** *The Aeneid,* Book II

Aphrodite's Plea

Aeneas, why this madness?
  What kindles this bitter flame?
Smother it before it burns
  us both. If your great name
means anything, set her free.
  Why tell her to "look around"
when you're the one who cannot see?
  This blood upon the ground,
it wasn't shed for Helen.
  Look, yourself, my boy,
at what immortal hands have wrought.
  The gods have toppled Troy!
There, amid the smoke and dust,
  Athena's shadow falls.
Queen Hera storms the Trojan gates;
  Poseidon shakes the walls.

Above us, Zeus the Thunderer
   rips apart the tower.
Save yourself! What mortal stands
   a chance against such power?
Quickly, son—I promise you,
   I'll never leave your side—
now, before the sun is up.
   A ship waits in the tide.

Cassandra, Priam's daughter, hair disheveled,
was dragged from the temple, from Athena's
shrine, and her eyes were raised to heaven—
her eyes, for chains held fast her gentle hands.
    —**Virgil**, *The Aeneid*, Book II

Cassandra's Prayer

Phoebus Apollo,
light of the heavens,
strike with your blinding hand!
Scorch me to cinders;
scatter my ashes
across our vanquished land.
Behold your priestess,
faithful Cassandra,
dragged like a beast to the bow
of a tossing ship,
to be wed at spear point.
How could you let them—how?

You swore to protect me—Sun God, I beg you,
help me! I'd rather die
than belong to that blood-stained brute,
Agamemnon. Apollo, can you deny
the promise you made me?
Lord, you'd betray me?
Strike with your blinding hand!
Scorch me to cinders—
scatter my ashes
across our vanquished land.

Nearby, beside the gates, for any to look upon
who has the heart, she lies face upward, Hecuba
weeping for the multitudes her multitude of tears.
—**Euripides,** *The Trojan Women,* 415 B.C.

Queen Hecuba's Song for Troy

Rise from the dust, old head;
begin your bleak refrain
of loss too great to measure,
of deathless pain.

Rise from the dust, old heart,
dancing to Death's grim beat.
Keep time to the dreaded song
with pounding feet.

Rise from the dust, old limbs,
clinging to Earth's cold bed
where Troy lies fallen,
her children dead.

> Where she stood
> the spot is called 'The Dog' and it is said
> (because of ancient wrongs) her voice still howls. . . .
> —**Ovid,** *The Metamorphoses,* Book XIII

A Greek Soldier's Report

I know what I saw, Odysseus;
  these eyes did not deceive.
You sent us to the women's tent,
  your orders, to retrieve
old Hecuba, King Priam's wife.
  We found the captives crying,
faces ashen, clothing torn,
  chanting, "The queen is dying."
They pointed toward the citadel,
  at freshly mounded graves
that held the House of Priam's dead.
  We followed the weeping slaves
and heard a woman's high-pitched wail—
  such pain I can't forget.
A human cry, and yet a mongrel's
  shadowed silhouette
was seen behind the dusty spire
  of broken bricks and stones

erected several days ago
   to cover Priam's bones.
The black-robed women, arms outstretched,
   entreated the crouching form.
It wailed again, then loped away.
   They followed in a swarm
like shrieking bats, their tattered clothes
   flapping in the breeze,
pleading and calling Hecuba's name.
   We thought it best to seize
the frenzied slaves before they tried
   to harm themselves, but now
I'm not so sure. They might have helped
   us find the queen. Somehow

she disappeared—vanished from
    the Earth. The only trace
our soldiers found of Hecuba
      was at the very place
   the doglike phantom first appeared,
      beside King Priam's tomb.
Her robes, the royal insignia,
      a lingering perfume—
it's all she left there, that's the truth.
      Whatever you believe,
I know what I saw, Odysseus.
      These eyes did not deceive.

Cassandra's Freedom Chant

My
  body's
   a flame
   rippling
the air;
    my mind,
    a cool breeze.
  It takes me where
  I want—so far,
 so far from here,
from crush of chain,
 from prod of spear
 and plunging bow,
where torch's light
   illuminates this
   marriage rite,
   so high, high
   above the sea,
    so far away.
      I'll always be
        a rippling flame,
          so bright
            I'll see
            forever,
            higher,
            farther,
            free.

Helen

That story is not true.
You [Helen] never sailed in the benched ships.
You never went to the city of Troy.
—Thought to be written by the poet **Stesichorus**
in his *Palinode*, sixth century B.C.

Tell the World

Helen Speaks

Poet, you defend me?
  Who takes a woman's side?
With Troy in ashes, sacrificed
  to my husband's wounded pride,
the world cries out in one loud voice,
  "Helen—she's to blame!"
How can it be? I was nothing more
  than a pawn in the goddesses' game.
    Who speaks for Helen? Will you dare
    tell the world I wasn't there?

Poet, you believe me?
  So many thought they'd seen
this famous face in Troy—I tell you,
  that was a phantom queen,

an impostor sent by Hera,
   who took me to Egypt land
and hid me there for ten long years
   to foil Aphrodite's plan.
     I set no foot in Troy, I swear.
     Tell the world.
       I wasn't there.

Yet portents of the Gods on Earth or Heaven
Cannot delay the hour of Fate upon us. . . .
—**Ovid,** *The Metamorphoses,* Book XV

Epilogue: Questioning the Muse

POET: Tell us, muse, what really caused
              this ancient devastation;
          did one man's act of love, alone,
              destroy the Trojan nation?

MUSE: *The fall of Troy is written*
              on tablets of tempered steel,
          its legend deeply etched,
              guarded with deathless zeal
          by three gray-haired sisters,
              goddesses who wield
          indomitable power.
              Even Zeus must yield
          to Clothos, who spins the thread
              clear-eyed Lachesis measures,
          each strand a life that Atropos,
              their dreaded sister, severs.

POET: Help us, muse, to understand
            the riddles you employ;
         tell us what these seamstress sisters
            meant to fabled Troy.

MUSE: *The length and breadth of human life*
            is governed by three Fates—
         sisters who hold all knowledge
            of past and future dates.
         No god can change the sharp-cut words
            on Time's enduring table.
         Poet—seek what's written there,
            the truth behind the fable.

So Menelaus traveled to Egypt, and on his arrival
sailed up the river [Nile] as far as Memphis, and related
all that had happened. He was given rich gifts of hospitality,
and received Helen back unharmed. . . .

—**Herodotus,** historian, fifth century B.C.

Appendix

Achilles (uh-KILL-eez):

Son of Thetis, a Nereid or sea goddess, and the mortal Peleus, he was one of the greatest Greek heroes of the Trojan War. He had a violent temper, which caused suffering to the Greeks as well as the Trojans. His grief over the death of his childhood friend, Patroklos, sent him into a rage that ended with the Trojan hero Hector's death. Achilles died soon after Hector; he was fatally wounded in the heel with a poisoned arrow shot by Hector's brother Paris. When Achilles was a child, his mother sought to make him immortal by immersing him in the river Styx. She held him under the water by his ankle, which remained untouched by the sacred river and therefore vulnerable to attack.

Aegean Sea (uh-JEE-un):

Part of the Mediterranean Sea between Greece and ancient Troy, now Turkey, bordered on the south by the island of Crete.

Aeneas (ih-NEE-us):

Son of the goddess Aphrodite and the mortal Anchises, he was a famous Trojan leader. He escaped the siege of Troy and eventually founded the city of Rome.

Agamemnon (ag-uh-MEM-non):
King of Argos, brother of Menelaus, and brother-in-law of Helen, he was commander-in-chief of the Greeks during the Trojan War. A brutal, arrogant man, he was intent on victory and personal gain at any cost.

Andromache (an-DROM-uh-kee):
Wife of Hector, she became a captive of the Greeks after the fall of Troy. The victorious Greeks put her infant son to death.

Aphrodite (af-ruh-DYE-tee):
Goddess of love and mother of the Trojan hero Aeneas, she fought with Hera and Athena over the Apple of Discord. Paris awarded the apple to her in exchange for obtaining Helen as his bride. Helen's abduction resulted in the Trojan War. Aphrodite aided the Trojans and was even wounded on the battlefield.

Apollo (uh-POLL-oh):
God of light, intellect, medicine, and the arts, he aided the Trojans throughout the ten-year siege. He loved the Trojan priestess Cassandra and gave her the ability to see the future, but she refused his advances. As punishment, he decreed that no one would ever believe her prophecies.

Ares (AIR-eez):
Arrogant, brutal son of Zeus and Hera and god of war, he was

hated by most of the other Olympians: He aided the Trojans but fled the battlefield and sought the protection of Zeus after he was wounded by Diomedes.

Artemis (AR-tuh-muss):
Goddess of the hunt, sister of Apollo.

Athena (uh-THEE-nuh):
Daughter of Zeus, goddess of wisdom, the arts, and the strategies of war, she fought on the side of the Greeks throughout the conflict.

Aulis (AW-lis):
The place of assembly of the Greek war fleet, before it sailed to Troy.

Calchas (KAL-kuss):
A seer who accompanied the Greeks during the Trojan War and prophesied their victory after a ten-year struggle.

Cassandra (kuh-SAN-druh):
Daughter of King Priam, sister of Hector and Paris, and priestess of Apollo, she foretold the fall of Troy.

Demeter (dih-ME-ter):
Goddess of the harvest, agriculture, and fertility.

Diomedes (dye-oh-ME-deez):
One of the greatest Greek heroes of the Trojan War. He wounded Ares and Aphrodite; fought both Hector and Aeneas; and, with Odysseus, stole the Palladium from the Trojan temple.

Dionysus (dye-oh-NIGH-suss):
God of wine and fertility.

Epeios (eh-PEE-us):
Greek warrior credited by Homer in *The Odyssey* as being the architect and builder of the Trojan horse.

Eris (EAR-iss):
Goddess of discord, or strife, and sister of Ares, she is famous for instigating a quarrel among the goddesses gathered at the wedding of Thetis and Peleus. She threw a golden apple inscribed "for the fairest" among the wedding guests, which was claimed by Hera, Athena, and Aphrodite. The incident caused the Trojan War.

Fates (FAYTS):
Three Goddesses who were thought to control the destinies of mortals. They were: Lachesis, who assigned individuals their fates at birth; Clothos, who spun the thread of life; and Atropos, who cut it.

Hector (HECK-ter):

King Priam's oldest son and Troy's greatest warrior, he led the Trojans in battle against the Greeks. He killed many, including Patroklos, Achilles' childhood friend. Athena tricked Hector into facing Achilles alone on the battlefield, where the raging Achilles struck Hector with his spear. Achilles, mad with grief over the death of his friend, tied Hector's body to the back of his chariot and dragged the dead hero around the walls of Troy for several days.

Hecuba (HECK-you-buh):

Queen of Troy, wife of King Priam, mother of Cassandra, Hector, and Paris.

Helen (HELL-un):

Daughter of Zeus and Leda, wife of King Menelaus of Sparta, she was carried off by Paris to Troy. Her husband and his brother Agamemnon, King of Argos, assembled their Greek allies at Aulis and set sail for Troy to recover Helen. The Trojan War lasted ten years.

Hera: (HEAR-uh):

Wife of Zeus and second only to him among the Olympians, she lost the contest for the golden apple to Aphrodite.

Hermes (HUR-meez):

God of commerce and invention; patron god of travelers,

merchants, and thieves; Zeus's messenger who had wings on his heels and escorted people to Hades, the land of the dead.

Iris (EYE-riss):
Goddess of the rainbow and the gods' messenger.

Ithaca (ITH-uh-kuh):
A Greek island in the Ionian Sea and the legendary home of Odysseus.

Laocoön (lay-OCK-oh-on):
Son of King Priam chosen to be a priest of Poseidon. He spoke out against bringing the wooden horse into Troy. He and his two young sons were devoured by sea monsters shortly afterward.

Menelaus (men-uh-LAY-us):
King of Sparta, brother of Agamemnon, and husband of Helen, he and his Greek allies defeated the Trojans after ten years of warfare.

Mount Ida (EYE-duh):
Mountain in Troy where Paris lived as a shepherd.

Mount Olympus (oh-LIM-pus):
Mountain in Greece, legendary home of the gods.

Muse (MUZE):
Any of the nine daughters of Zeus and Mnemosyne (goddess of

memory), each of whom presided over a different art or science. The muses are considered to be the source of inspiration for poets, musicians, and artists.

Nereus (NEAR-ee-us):
Ancient god of the sea, father of the fifty sea goddesses called Nereids.

Odysseus (oh-DEE-see-us):
King of Ithaca, husband of Penelope, and one of the most well-known characters in Greek mythology. He was an ally of Menelaus and Agamemnon and a reluctant but distinguished participant in the Trojan War. One of the greatest Greek warriors, he was considered to be very shrewd and became an eloquent and persuasive leader of the Greek army at Troy.

Palladium (puh-LAY-dee-um):
A wooden image of Athena that is said to have fallen from heaven and was kept in her temple in Troy. As long as the Palladium remained within the walls of Troy, the city could not be defeated. Odysseus and Diomedes stole the statue in the tenth year of the conflict; Troy fell soon afterward.

Paris (PAIR-iss):
Son of King Priam, he was banished at birth because of his mother's prophetic dream that her son would bring doom to Troy. He lived as a shepherd on Mount Ida until he was called on to

judge which of three Olympian goddesses was the most beautiful. Paris chose the goddess Aphrodite because she promised he could marry Helen, who was considered the loveliest woman in the world. Paris fought in the Trojan War but preferred archery to the fierce hand-to-hand combat that characterized much of the conflict. He was not a respected leader like his brother Hector, who despised Paris for his indifference to the Trojans' plight and for instigating the war in the first place. He was credited with slaying Achilles. However, several sources say it was really Apollo disguised as Paris who shot the fatal arrow.

Patroklos (puh-TROE-kluss):
Achilles' closest friend, he was killed by Hector. Wild with grief and fury, Achilles entered the battle and killed Hector.

Penelope (puh-NELL-uh-pee):
Wife of Odysseus.

Persephone (purr-SEF-uh-nee):
Daughter of the goddess Demeter and unhappy wife of Hades, god of the dead.

Philoctetes (fih-LOCK-tuh-teez):
Archer who inherited the invincible bow and arrows of Hercules, he fought for the Greeks during the Trojan War. He killed Paris with one of his arrows and helped win the final victory.

Poseidon (poe-SIGH-dun):
Brother of Zeus and Hades, god of all oceans and earthquakes, he supported the Greeks throughout the Trojan War. He often disguised himself and went through the ranks of Greek soldiers, stirring their courage and urging them on to battle.

Priam (PRYE-um):
King of Troy and father of fifty sons and daughters, including Hector, Paris, Laocoön, and Cassandra. He was killed when Troy fell to the Greeks.

Pyrrhus (PIH-russ):
Bloodthirsty son of Achilles who fought in the Trojan War. He brutally killed King Priam and several of Priam's children during the final invasion of Troy.

Sinon (SIGH-non):
Greek youth who convinced the Trojans that the Greeks had fled Troy and were returning to their homeland. He tricked the Trojans into hauling the wooden horse within Troy's walls by telling them it was an offering to the goddess Athena. Sinon further convinced Priam that if the Trojans managed to pull the horse within their gates, they would gain Athena's patronage.

Sparta (SPAR-tuh):
Greek city-state renowned for military prowess and for the disciplined, austere lifestyle of its inhabitants.

Thetis (THEE-tiss):
A Nereid, she was one of the daughters of Ocean, the wife of the mortal Peleus, and the mother of Achilles. She petitioned Zeus on behalf of her son, who sought revenge for his mistreatment by the Greek commander, Agamemnon.

Troy (TROI):
Wealthy but ill-fated city in Troas, northwestern Asia Minor (present-day Turkey). Site of the Trojan War.

Zeus (ZOOSS):
Supreme ruler of the Olympian gods, he tried to remain neutral during the Trojan War but was drawn into the struggle by the Nereid Thetis, mother of Achilles. Because of Achilles' quarrel with the Greek commander, Agamemnon, Thetis asked Zeus to assist the Trojans. She hoped to punish the Greeks for Agamemnon's ill treatment of her son. Zeus agreed, knowing that the Greeks would eventually win the struggle because the outcome had already been ordained by the Fates.

Bibliography

Casson, Lionel, editor and translator. *Selected Satires of Lucian*.
New York: W. W. Norton & Company, Inc., 1968.

Finley, M. I., editor. *The Portable Greek Historians*. New York:
Penguin Books, 1977.

Gregory, Horace, translator. *Ovid, The Metamorphoses*. New York:
Mentor Books, Penguin Group, 1960.

Grene, David, and Richmond Lattimore, editors. *Greek Tragedies*,
Vols. 1–2. Chicago: University of Chicago Press, 1960.

Lattimore, Richmond, translator. *The Iliad of Homer*. Chicago:
University of Chicago Press, 1961.

Lattimore, Richmond, translator. *The Odyssey of Homer*. New York:
Perennial Classics, HarperCollins Publishers, 1999.

Mandelbaum, Allen, translator. *The Aeneid of Virgil*. New York:
Bantam Books, 1985.